KING OF KINGS

SUSAN HILL

illustrated by John Lawrence

CANDLEWICK PRESS
CAMBRIDGE, MASSACHUSETTS

Mr. Hegarty hadn't always been alone. And being alone didn't always mean being lonely. But quite often it did.

Once, there had been Mrs. Hegarty, whose name had been Doll, or sometimes Dolly, and they had been married for a great many years, and there had been good days and bad days but mostly good, some ups and some downs, but mostly ups, and the great many years had not seemed nearly enough before Mrs. Hegarty got ill and then very much iller, and died. So that now there was only

Mr. Hegarty and Cat the cat, and Jacko.

Cat the cat had never been bought or in any other way chosen, he had just come —one day onto the wall, the next day in the yard, the third day into the house, and after that, as Mr. Hegarty said, paws under the table for good.

Cat, like all cats, came and went as he pleased. But Jacko had been chosen all right, for his black-patch eye and his brave, bright bark, and for being cheap from the man with the cart in the lane, because his legs were bandy.

Mr. Hegarty's house was the last in the street. After it came the wharves and warehouses, the empty lot and the church, the building site, the road, and the railway.

But walk another way and there were still a few streets left. Though not the street where Mr. Hegarty was born and grew to be a man, nor the one where Mrs. Hegarty had been born and got married from, all those years ago. They are gone, and their neighbors' houses too, and the pub and the shop on the

corner, pulled down in heaps of dust and rubble and carted away on trucks.

There were cranes now, and site offices, concrete girders and craters in the ground, men in hard hats and machines, judder-judder, all day, all day.

But walk a bit farther still, which Mr. Hegarty and Jacko always did, and there was the Lane, just as it had always been, and the streets and squares around it, and shops and buses and flats and people, schools and churches, the bit of park and the King's Hospital.

And now it was Christmas Eve. Mr. Hegarty had been about all day. He liked to be about. He liked Christmas Eve. Everybody talked to everybody else and there was a lot of bustle; people were cheerful. He'd been about the market, among the stalls and carts. Then, he and Jacko had stood for a long time on the corner, just for the pleasure of watching everything. He'd had his dinner out—pie and chips—and his tea, with a mince pie "on the house." Lotta, who kept the café, had said, "because ees Christmas."

But now it was late. Dark. Now, everything was closing down. They were sweeping up around the carts, sprigs of holly and paper from the oranges and a few lost Brussels sprouts.

"Good night then. Happy Christmas."
Lamps out. Blinds up. Shutters down.

The main road was jammed. The trains went along the line, full of everyone going home. So Mr. Hegarty and Jacko went home too. Across the building site. Quiet now, the great crane still and silent. It had a Christmas tree balanced on the very end, with lights and decorations. But the men had finished at dinnertime today.

Past the warehouses and wharves. Once, Mr. Hegarty had been a nightwatchman on the wharf. That was when the ships had docked, years ago. There were no ships now.

Across the last bit of the empty lot. Jacko's ears twitched.

Home.

Christmas Eve. The wind blew down alleyways, across the dark wharves, smelling of rain and river. No snow. No star. But Christmas Eve isn't often like the stories.

Mr. Hegarty reached home. There was a carrier bag on the step, with three wrapped-up presents inside, and a card. "To Mr. Hegarty and Jacko and Cat, a Happy Christmas, with love from Jo."

Jo and his family lived next door. But they had gone away that morning, to stay with his grandmother for the holiday. One day, they'd go away altogether. Everybody would. This was the last street. Mr. Hegarty didn't want to think about it.

Nothing inside the house had changed very much since he and Mrs. Hegarty moved in, newly married; and since Mrs. Hegarty died, nothing had changed at all. Mr. Hegarty wanted it like that, just as it was and had always been and as she had left it.

He kept it clean and put things away in the same old places and polished the windows and blackened the hearth and washed up in the stone sink and slept in the big brass bed.

And every Christmas, he put up the decorations, around the pictures and over the mirror and along the mantelpiece, with a wreath of holly on the front door, just as Mrs. Hegarty always had.

It was very quiet. Mr. Hegarty went into the scullery to wash his hands, then fed Jacko and Cat, put the kettle on, made up the fire, and sat beside it. And Mrs. Hegarty sat beside him, smiling out from the silver photograph frame on the little table.

Later, the band came and played "Silent Night" and "Hark, the Herald Angels," under the orange lamp at the end of the street, and the man with the collecting tin came down to Mr. Hegarty's door and they had a chat. Then, they played one more carol, which was "In the Bleak Midwinter," because it had been Mrs. Hegarty's favorite, before they went away. But for quite a while, the strains of trumpet and tuba and cornet, "O Little Town of Bethlehem" and "While Shepherds Watched" floated faintly back to him across the wharves and the empty lot. Then, it was quiet again.

For the rest of the evening, while Jacko and Cat slept on the hearth rug, Mr. Hegarty sat in his armchair, thinking, as people do, of other Christmases, good and bad and in-between—but mostly good, for times past are golden in the memory to an old and lonely man.

At ten o'clock, he got up, and Jacko ran to the front door, and they went for their last walk, up the street and down again. There was nobody about, though some of the houses had lights on, glowing behind curtains, and two

of them had Christmas trees in the windows.

And the wind still blew, down the alleyways and across the wharves and the empty lot, with the smell of the river on its breath.

Christmas Eve. Mr. Hegarty's heart lifted. It was still special, after all, there was no getting away from that. Then, he let Cat out, locked up, wound his watch, and went upstairs to bed.

Sometime after midnight, he woke again. At first, he didn't know why. There was no sound, except for Jacko, snoring softly.

Then, there was something, a very faint, distant sound, not inside the house, out. Mr. Hegarty put on his slippers, went downstairs, and opened the front door.

Everything was still. It had stopped raining and the wind had died down.

The moon shone.

Jacko came pattering down the stairs and stopped beside Mr. Hegarty at the front door.

There it was again. Very faint. A mewling sound. Kittens?

Mr. Hegarty put on his coat and shoes and took the flashlight. Then, he went out of the house and across the empty lot, toward the church. Jacko ran ahead, ears cocked, tail up.

There were railings around the old church, but the padlock on the gate was broken. The sound was louder. Mr. Hegarty stopped. The moon came out again from behind a cloud. Jacko had trotted up the weed-covered path to the church porch and Mr. Hegarty could see him standing beside something, wagging his tail. So he went too.

Here, the sound was loud and clear and unmistakable.

Mr. Hegarty shone his flashlight.

On a ledge inside the dark, damp, cold stone porch of the church, stood a shallow cardboard box.

Inside the box lay a baby. It was very small, and wrapped in a scruffy piece of blanket.

"Now then!" said Mr. Hegarty softly. "Now then."

But then he didn't know quite what to do.

He and Mrs. Hegarty had never had any children. Mr. Hegarty had never even held a baby. In his own home, there had been seven children, but as he had been the youngest, all the others had picked him up.

The moon went behind a cloud again, and the baby stopped crying and just lay. Jacko sat, waiting.

"Well," said Mr. Hegarty.

And then, because there was nothing else that he could do, he picked up the box with the baby in it, very gently. And as he did so, he remembered that it was not Christmas Eve any longer, but Christmas Day.

Then, carrying the box very carefully, he made his way slowly out of the church porch, and back across the empty lot, Jacko trotting at his heels. He couldn't hold the flashlight as well, so he put it at the bottom of the box, by the baby's feet.

Up the street, past the building site and the wharves and warehouses—empty and silent—toward the streets, and then the market, the shops, the Lane. His footsteps echoed.

The pubs and cafés had long since shut. The last trains had gone, and there were no cars on the main road.

Mr. Hegarty walked on, stopping now and then to set the box down and rest his arms.

Then Jacko stopped too, and waited patiently.

The baby had gone to sleep.

From across the last square, beside the bit of park, Mr. Hegarty could see the lights shining out.

"Now then," he said. But then, just for a minute, he didn't want to go on, didn't want to let the baby go. He felt a strange, half-sad, half-angry feeling, like a knot tightening inside him. Whoever could have left it in a box, in a cold porch, at Christmas? He looked down at it again. But then, because he knew there was only one, right thing to do, he crossed the road and walked up the drive to the entrance.

"Stay," he said. Jacko stayed.

Then, Mr. Hegarty went through the glass doors into the lighted entrance of the King's Hospital.

In the hall, there was a huge Christmas tree, and paper chains and decorations strung from the ceiling and all around the walls. At the far end was a reception desk, with a porter behind it, and a nurse standing beside. Mr. Hegarty went up to them and stood, holding the box in his arms.

"I've brought a baby," he said.

In the next hour or so, a lot of things happened. The baby was taken away, and Mr. Hegarty asked to sit down and answer a great many questions, from a nurse, and a doctor, and finally, from two policemen. They brought him a cup of tea, and then another, with a pink bun, and asked him to sign some papers, and the whole time, Jacko sat without moving or barking, on the step beyond the glass doors.

But in the end, the nurse came back again and said, "You can go now, Mr. Hegarty. You must be tired out."

"Right," said the policemen. "We'll drop you off. Trafalgar Street, isn't it?"

Mr. Hegarty stood up. He was tired, tired enough to drop, and muddled and in a way, sad.

"No, thank you very much," he said. "If it's all the same to you, I'll walk." And he went slowly across the blue carpet to the glass doors, where Jacko was waiting.

"Come on then," Mr. Hegarty said. Jacko came.

He did sleep, just a bit, but it was a strange, restless sleep, full of odd dreams and noises.

When he woke properly, it was just coming light. Gray. Damp looking. "Happy Christmas, Jacko," Mr. Hegarty said. Jacko hardly stirred.

He was going to make a pot of tea, and then open his present from Jo. But, as he washed, he knew that he wouldn't, not yet. Knew that he would have to go there first, straight away, because the baby had been on his mind all night, and he couldn't settle until he'd made sure about it.

He let Cat in, whistled to Jacko, and crossed the street, all over again, in the same direction as before.

And as he walked, he wondered. Whose baby? When? How? Why? What would happen to it now?

He hadn't even found out what it was, girl or boy, hadn't liked to ask.

The hospital looked different in the early morning light, larger, grayer, somehow less friendly.

But he left Jacko on the step again, and went in, down the blue carpet.

After he had explained, they left him, sitting on a chair in a corridor. The hospital was still quiet, but not like the night before. He could hear doors banging and the elevator going up and down. Perhaps they would bring him a cup of tea again. He always had one as soon as he got up. He was missing it now.

But it didn't really matter. He'd had to come.

"Mr. Hegarty?"

Mr. Hegarty stood up.

"Would you like to come with me?"

Through doors. Down a corridor.

"I'm sure you'd like to see him wouldn't you?"

Him. A boy then. Yes, that was as it should be.

"He's fine, thanks to you. But if you hadn't found him . . . "

They went down more corridors. Around corners. Through doors. Stopped.

"You'll see that we've done something special," she said.

"We always wait for the first baby born in the hospital on Christmas Day, but there hadn't been one yet. And besides, we thought that your baby was the most important one here today. Come in and see."

There were babies in small cribs. Through a glass window, he could see beds.

"Look, Mr. Hegarty."

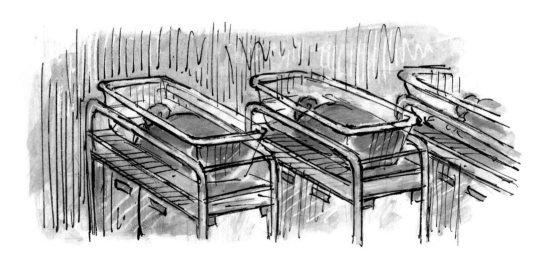

At the end of the room, on a small, raised platform, stood a crib, draped and decorated, under a canopy. Hanging above the canopy was a star. "The Christmas crib," she said. "Only used once a year. Today."

Mr. Hegarty went a step closer. Looked down. And there he was, the baby from the cardboard box in the dark church porch, the baby he had found and carried here with Jacko. The Christmas baby.

For a while, Mr. Hegarty didn't speak.

Then he said quietly, "King of Kings. That's who he is. The King of Kings." And went, smiling, out of the nursery.

They did find him a cup of tea, and a breakfast too, and a plate of sausages for Jacko, and said they would be letting him know what happened to the baby, when there was any news.

"And you'll be welcome to come and see him you know," the nurse said. "Any day."

"Thank you," Mr. Hegarty said. "Thank you very much. I should like that."

And then he went home, with Jacko trotting beside him, through the quiet early streets of Christmas morning.